The Twelve Rabbids of Christmas

illustrated by Patrick Spaziante

Simon Spotlight
New York London Toronto Sydney New Delhi

SIMON SPOTLIGHT/NICKELODEON
An imprint of Simon & Schuster Children's Publishing Division
1230 Avenue of the Americas. New York. New York 10020
This Simon Spotlight edition September 2014 © 2014 Ubisoft
Entertainment. All rights reserved. Rabbids. Ubisoft. and the
Ubisoft logo are trademarks of Ubisoft Entertainment in the
U.S. and/or other countries. All rights reserved. including
the right of reproduction in whole or in part in any form.
SIMON SPOTLIGHT and colophon are registered trademarks
of Simon & Schuster. Inc. For information about
special discounts for bulk purchases. please contact
Simon & Schuster Special Sales at 1-866-506-1949
or business@simonandschuster.com.
Manufactured in the United States of America
0814 LAK
First Edition 10 9 8 7 6 5 4 3 2 1
ISBN 978-1-4814-2032-7
ISBN 978-1-4814-2033-4 (eBook)

On the first day of Christmas, the Rabbids gave to me a headache and a skinned knee.

On the second day of Christmas,
the Rabbids gave to me
two barking pugs,
and a headache and a skinned knee.

On the third day of Christmas,
the Rabbids gave to me
three leaky pens, two barking pugs,
and a headache and a skinned knee.

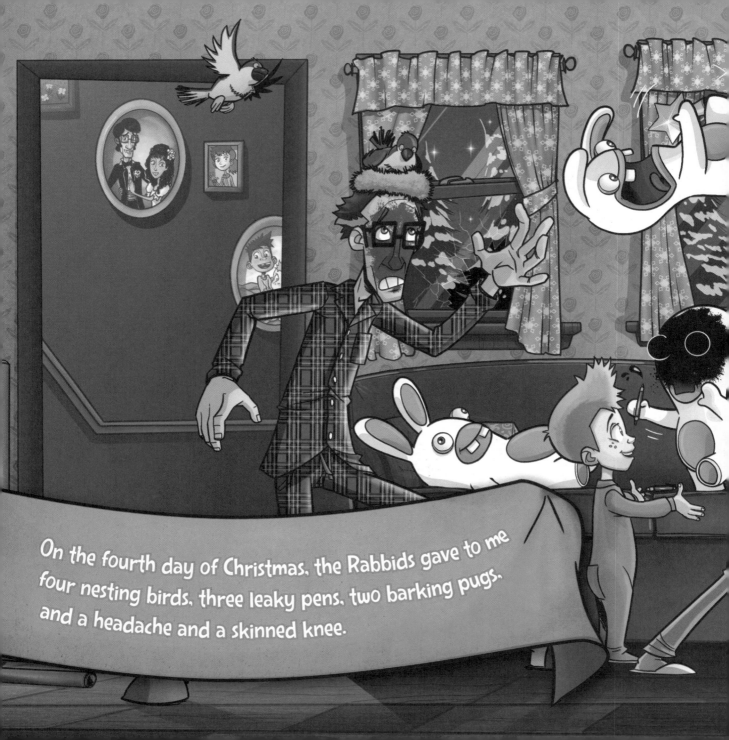

On the fourth day of Christmas, the Rabbids gave to me four nesting birds, three leaky pens, two barking pugs, and a headache and a skinned knee.

On the fifth day of Christmas, the Rabbids gave to me FIVE GOLDEN SLINGS, four nesting birds, three leaky pens, two barking pugs, and a headache and a skinned knee.

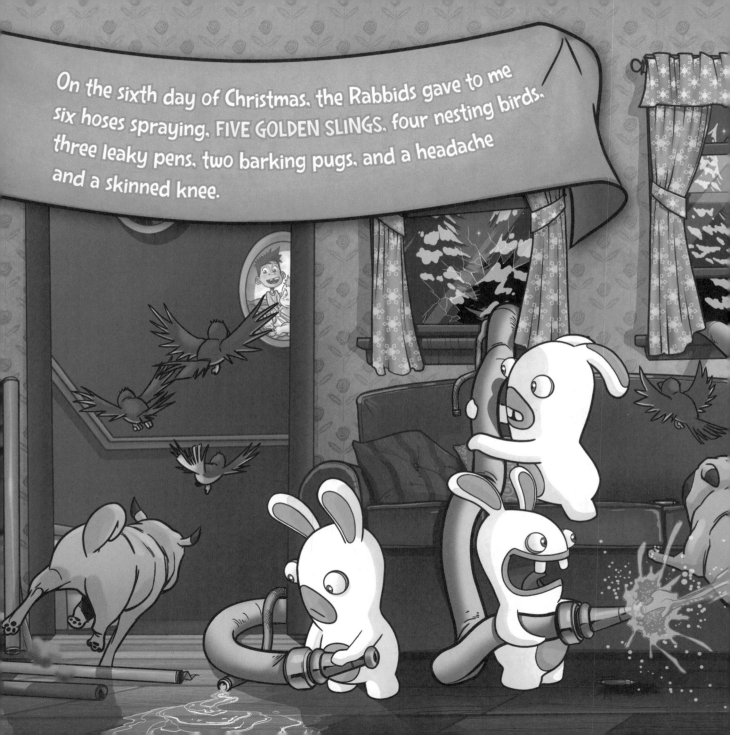

On the sixth day of Christmas, the Rabbids gave to me six hoses spraying, FIVE GOLDEN SLINGS, four nesting birds, three leaky pens, two barking pugs, and a headache and a skinned knee.

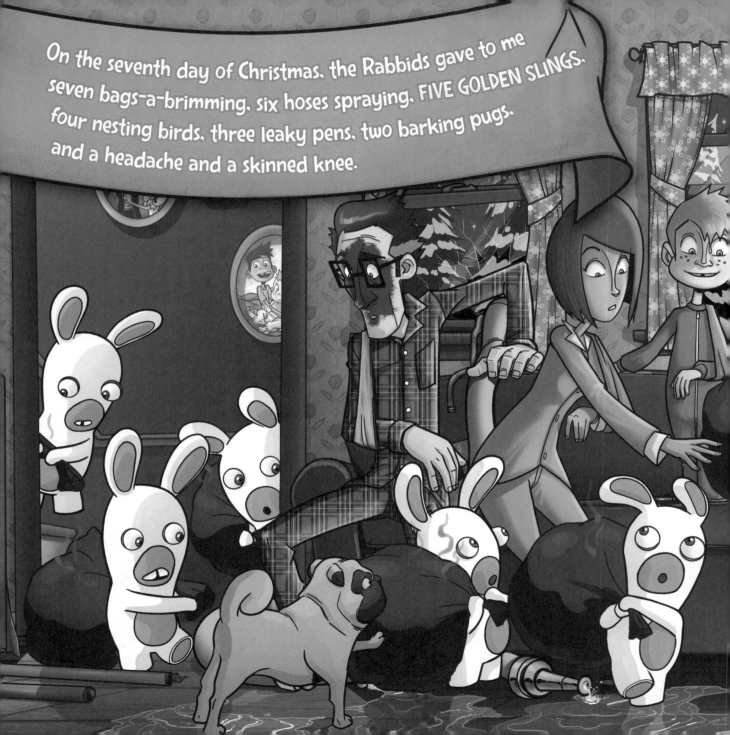

On the seventh day of Christmas, the Rabbids gave to me seven bags-a-brimming, six hoses spraying, FIVE GOLDEN SLINGS, four nesting birds, three leaky pens, two barking pugs, and a headache and a skinned knee.

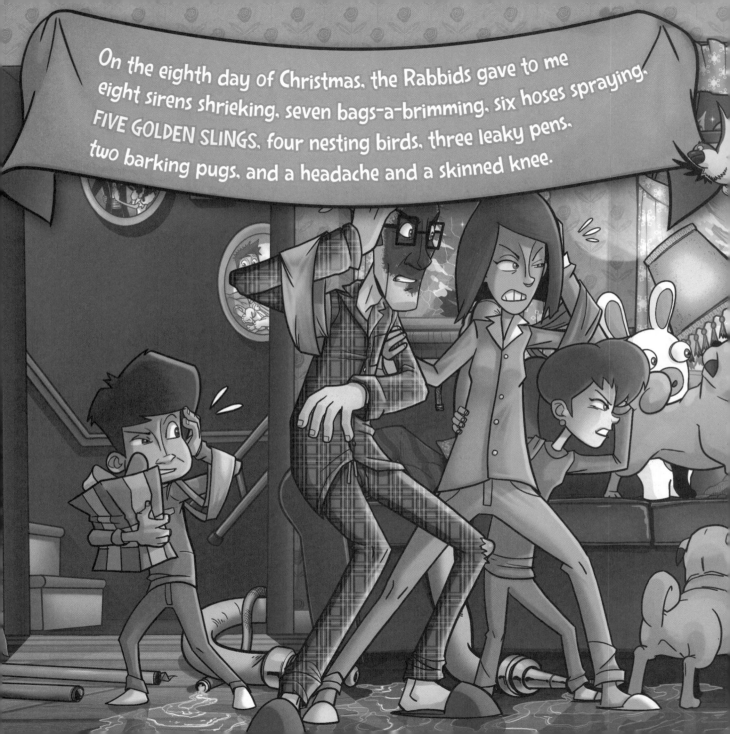

On the eighth day of Christmas, the Rabbids gave to me eight sirens shrieking, seven bags-a-brimming, six hoses spraying, FIVE GOLDEN SLINGS, four nesting birds, three leaky pens, two barking pugs, and a headache and a skinned knee.

On the ninth day of Christmas, the Rabbids gave to me nine grandpas farting, eight sirens shrieking, seven bags-a-brimming, six hoses spraying, FIVE GOLDEN SLINGS, four nesting birds, three leaky pens, two barking pugs, and a headache and a skinned knee.

On the tenth day of Christmas, the Rabbids gave to me ten babies burping, nine grandpas farting, eight sirens shrieking, seven bags-a-brimming, six hoses spraying, FIVE GOLDEN SLINGS, four nesting birds, three leaky pens, two barking pugs, and a headache and a skinned knee.

On the eleventh day of Christmas, the Rabbids gave to me eleven robbers robbing, ten babies burping, nine grandpas farting, eight sirens shrieking, seven bags-a-brimming, six hoses spraying, FIVE GOLDEN SLINGS, four nesting birds, three leaky pens, two barking pugs, and a headache and a skinned knee.